This Book Belongs To:

As you read the book, see if you can spot the butterfly on each page.

To my children, Rebecca, and David, who have always inspired me. And to the many kitties I have loved in my lifetime. Even though Alastair is the only one to get his own book, the butterfly represents the spirit of all the other kitties that have been part of my family.

Special thanks to Katie Weaver, Frank Archer, Brooke Vitale, David Ramer, Aaron Zeitlin.

Publisher's Cataloging-in-Publication data

Names: Ramer, Valerie, author. | Harrington, Kat, illustrator.
Title: Alastair McAllister Goes to School / by Valerie Ramer ; illustrated by Kat Harrington.
Description: Edmonds, WA: Redwriting Books, 2021.
Summary: Alastair feels unwelcome at kitty-garten because he looks different from the other kittens, but they soon come to appreciate how special he is.

Identifiers:
LCCN: 2021900785
ISBN: 978-1-7365031-0-2 (Hardcover)
978-1-7365031-2-6 (pbk.)
978- 1-7365031-1-9 (ebook)

Subjects: LCSH Schools–Juvenile fiction. | Cats–Juvenile fiction.
Kittens–Juvenile fiction.| Self-esteem–Juvenile fiction.
Self-acceptance–Juvenile fiction. | CYAC Schools–Fiction.
Cats–Fiction. | Kittens–Fiction. | Self-esteem–Fiction.
Self-acceptance–Fiction. | BISAC JUVENILE FICTION / Animals / Cats
Classification: LCC PZ7.1.R359 Ala 2021 | DDC [E]–dc23

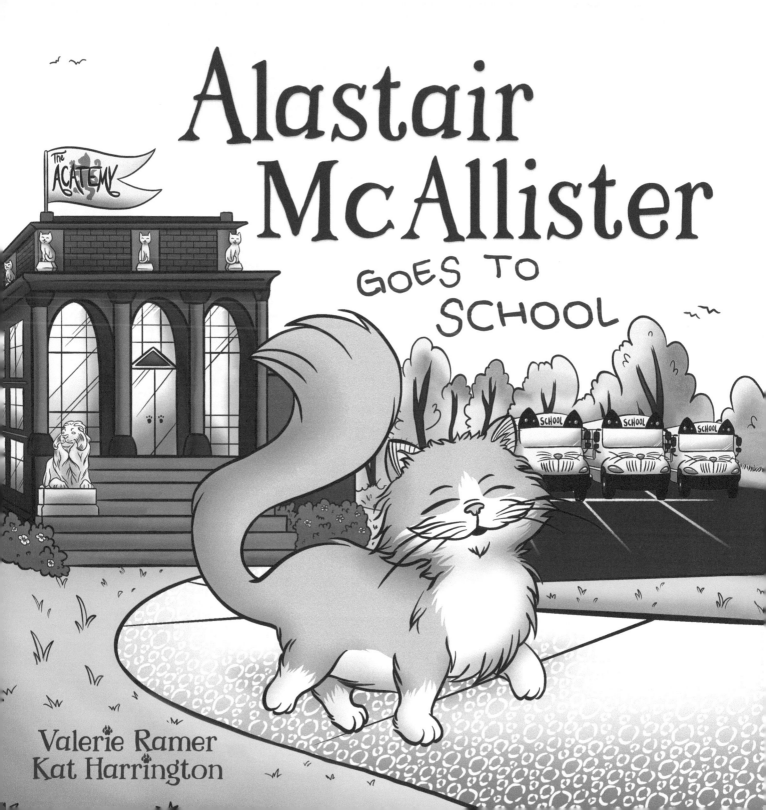

Alastair McAllister was **excited** for his ≫ **first** ≪ day of Kittygarten. It was going to be PURRFECT!

KITTYGARTEN BUS

School looked **SO big**.
Alastair felt very,
very small.

Alastair was **nervous** but **excited** to meet the other kittens.

Then **Alastair** heard **laughter**.
The kittens were **pointing** at him.

"Why is your **tail so fluffy?**"
asked a gray kitty named Tucker.

"Why is your **hair so long?**"
asked a black kitty
named Bentley.

"Why are your **eyes so big?**
Why is your **face so flat?**"
asked a kitty named Ollie,
giggling so hard
he fell over.

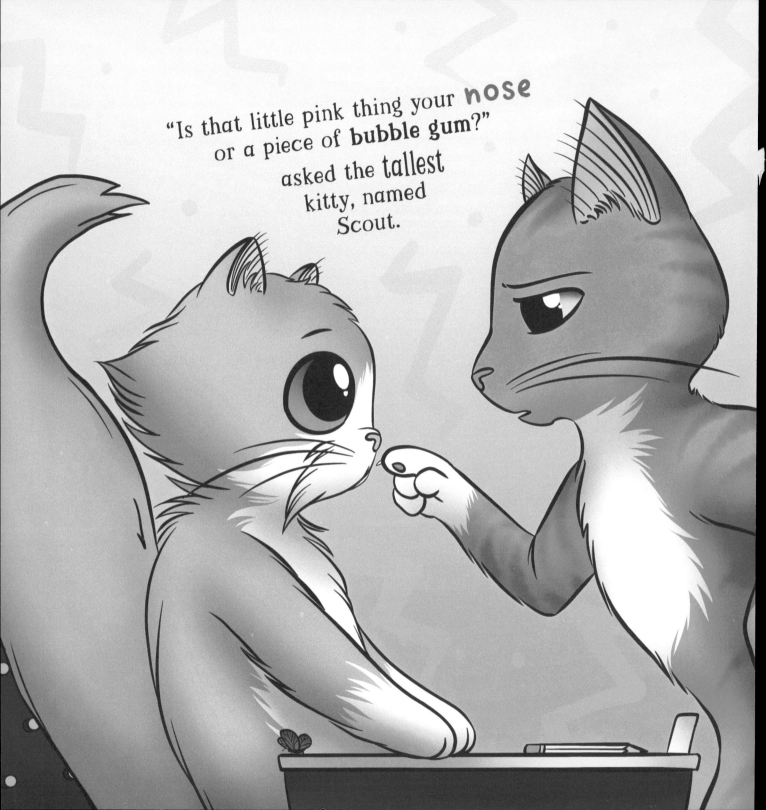

Alastair tried not to cry.
He didn't think his hair was too long or his face was **too flat**.
He *loved* his pink nose and especially his big fluffy tail.

Soon it was lunch time.

Alastair looked forward to using his ➤BRAND-NEW➤ lunch box.

He picked it out himself because it had a flat dish.

FISH CRACKER

SUPER Flat-Face lunchbox!

It was hard for him to eat from a bowl.
"What do you eat in that
flat thing, pancakes?"
asked Tucker.

Alastair tried, but the pieces of food went up his **nose**.

"I like my lunchbox better," he sighed.

He ate his lunch
alone.

At recess they **pounced** on leaves and played **mouseball**.

Alastair was having fun. He forgot about being **sad**.

Scout shouted, "Let's play hide-and-seek!" Alastair hid but was too easy to find. "Your tail is too fluffy," said Scout, "you can only play if you're IT!"

"I can't do *anything* right,"
he whispered to no one.

Alastair told
his Mommy
what happened.
"I'm not like the
other kittens."

"It's okay to be
different.
I love you just the
way you are."

Alastair wanted to fit in. That night, he had an **idea**.

The next morning, he snuck into Mommy's bathroom.

He tried a little dab of **this**... a little dab of **that**...

MANE TAMER

The other kittens arrived to play before school opened.

Suddenly, thunder BOOMED and rain poured down.

Scared, the kittens huddled together.

All except Alastair.

Alastair was **not afraid**. He *loved* water. Loud noises didn't scare him. He never ran from Mommy's vacuum cleaner.

"What's happening to **Alastair**?"

Alastair explained his tail was perfect for him and their tails were perfect for them. The kittens realized they shouldn't have teased **Alastair** for being different.

They were all
DIFFERENT
in their own way.

🐾 VALERIE RAMER

is **Alastair's** real-life Mommy. She is a strong advocate for animals. Valerie has raised two amazing human beings, Rebecca, and David, and lots of kittens. With a degree in theater from the American Academy of Dramatic Arts, NY, she has worked as an actress and talent agent. Her story telling skills were refined by ghost writing numerous TV and film screenplays. She also wrote and directed children's theatre around the Seattle area. *Alastair McAllister Goes to School* is her first children's book.

🐾 KAT HARRINGTON

is an illustrator from Omaha, NE who specializes in watercolor, ink, and digital illustrations. She has most notably illustrated for This Old House magazine and Bethany House books. When she is not creating art and daydreaming, she can be found enjoying time with her husband and three fur babies.

Alastair McAllister is a real exotic longhair cat.
This book is a creative expression of the relationships
he has with other cats.

For more information and pictures of the real **Alastair**
visit our website: www.Redwritingbooks.com

Printed in the USA
CPSIA information can be obtained
at www.ICGtesting.com
LVHW070956250823

755934LV00025B/225